The Christmas Time Travelers 3

RETURN TO BETHLEHEM

Written & Illustrated by:

L.M HAYNES

The Christmas Time Traveler 3: The Return to Bethlehem
Copyright © 2024 by L.M HAYNES

All rights reserved. No part of this publication may be reproduced, distributed, or transmitted in any form or by any means, including photocopying, recording, or other electronic or mechanical methods, without the prior written permission of the publisher or author, except in the case of brief quotations embodied in critical reviews and certain other noncommercial uses permitted by copyright law.

Although every precaution has been taken to verify the accuracy of the information contained herein, the author and publisher assume no responsibility for any errors or omissions. No liability is assumed for damages that may result from the use of information contained within.

ISBN-13: Paperback: 979-8-8691-8136-7
          ePub: 979-8-8691-8137-4
          Hardback: 979-8-8691-8140-4

Printed in the United States of America

PUBLISHING

The Christmas Time Travelers 3

Return to Bethlehem

WRITTEN AND ILLUSTRATED:
L.M HAYNES

The Christmas Time Travelers 3

Return to Bethlehem

Professor Malcolm McDougal and his four friends, Lily, Benji, Karat and Jem are preparing for a quiet, peaceful Christmas together in their hometown of Coventry. A headline in the local newspaper changes their plans, and once again the five friends find themselves on a journey back to the first Christmas. Before this journey ends, and before Christmas morning arrives, the professor will be reminded that everything we do should be done for the glory of God. With the help of his four furry and loyal friends and his amazing time machine, the wonderful Christmas story will forever stay a matter of faith.

Two years passed since Professor Malcolm McDougal, along with Lily, Benji, Karat and Jem took their unforgettable journey back to the first Christmas in the professor's time machine.

It was once again Christmas Eve in the tiny New England town of Coventry. The professor had every intention of keeping this Christmas as calm and peaceful as last year's.

There was a roaring fire crackling in the living room fireplace. The professor settled himself on the sofa with the daily newspaper, surrounded by his four beloved friends. Lily and Benji were puggles. Karat was a golden retriever, and Jem a precocious staffy bull terrier.

As the professor began to read the day's newspaper, he could hardly believe his eyes. The headline read:

"Remains of 21st Century Cellphone found in excavation outside of Bethlehem. Scientists believe this area has not seen the light of day for two-thousand years."

"How could this be?" worried the professor. "Is it possible that after all of these centuries, the cellphone that I buried there has been found?"

"This is terrible. The very reason that I left my phone behind will be forever ruined if any of the photos that I took can somehow be saved."

At that moment, Professor McDougal realized what had to be done. It was not going to be the calm and peaceful Christmas that he had imagined.

"The only way for me to keep my phone from being found, and for this newspaper headline to disappear, is for me to make another journey in my time machine and try to retrieve my cellphone," the professor thought out loud to himself.

He would take Lily, Benji, Karat and Jem along with him to help sniff out the spot where he buried his cellphone.

Without delay, the professor went into his bedroom closet and pulled out the shepherd's costume that he wore on his previous journey. He then went into his living room, swept away some of the dust that had gathered on his time machine and slowly opened the door.

All of the commotion that the professor was making caused his four friends to become quite unsettled, and they all wandered over to the time machine to see what was happening.

"Get ready my sweet friends," the professor announced. "In a few minutes we will all be taking another journey in time BACK TO BETHLEHEM!"

With that, the professor checked to make sure the windows and doors of his house were locked, and that the fire burning in the fireplace was extinguished. He left the Christmas tree lit to lift the spirit of any lonely passersby.

Lily, Benji, Karat and Jem were very hesitant as they entered the round, rusty brown time machine. After all, it had been two years since they last saw the inside of the professor's amazing invention.

Once inside, the professor joined them, closed the creaky door, set the necessary dials on the control panel and pressed the big, round start button.

Within moments, the time machine shook, lights flashed and the five friends found themselves on the same sandy hill outside of Bethlehem that they had visited two Christmases before.

Now, instead of the professor just having his four friends sniff out his cellphone and immediately return to the present, curiosity once again got the best of him.

"Please come with me Lily, Benji, Karat and Jem?" the professor asked. "I want to take one last look at the baby Jesus. After we do that, my heart will be full once again, and we can begin our search for my cellphone."

As the professor and his four friends began their walk to the main archway of Bethlehem, they were accompanied by many shepherds from the surrounding desert hills.

Once inside, they easily found their way to the stable where the child lay. After all, they had been there before. The professor brought Lily, Benji, Karat and Jem to a dark corner of the stable where they could just watch this blessed first Christmas from afar.

They all stood in silence for many minutes until something wonderful happened. Remembering her two previous visits to the first Christmas, Lily decided to get one more close up view of her friend Jesus.

She gently stepped out of the shadows from the corner of the stable, and walked very slowly toward the manger that was cradling the baby.

Lily recognized the little child and the powder blue blanket that he was wrapped in. As she reached the side of the manger, she gently lifted her head so she could take a closer look.

As she did, her tiny puggle face was filled with wonder at how beautiful the baby Jesus was. She stared at the baby until the professor came over to the manger and lead her away.

Once back in the shadows of the stable, the professor knelt down and gently spoke to Lily:

"We have to leave now my precious Lily. I understand that the baby Jesus is your friend and that you want to be near him, but we must find my cellphone and travel back to our home. It won't be long before the whole world finds out that this child was meant to be a friend and savior to us all. C'mon girl. Let's go!"

With that, Professor McDougal gathered his four friends together, they left Bethlehem behind and began what seemed like the impossible task of finding the professor's phone in the sands outside of Bethlehem.

    The professor could only hope that his time machine had left them off very near the same spot where he had buried his phone. It was time for Lily, Benji, Karat and Jem to go to work.

    As they walked from the archway of Bethlehem towards the spot in the desert where the professor believed he buried his phone, he saw a fading image of himself and his four friends off in the distance.

Lily, Benji, Karat and Jem had also seen the image, and began to run to the same spot. The professor kept up as best as he could.

By the time they all arrived at the same spot, the image completely disappeared.

"That image that we all saw was the five of us leaving Bethlehem two Christmases ago," the professor explained to his friends. "I bet we are standing very near the spot where I buried my phone. Start sniffing away my dear hearts!"

Professor McDougal then instructed his precious pups to begin sniffing near the area where the image disappeared. Lily, Benji, Karat and Jem began their frantic search for the professor's phone.

Each sniffed around in circles along the surface of the sand, but to no avail. After a number of minutes had passed, with no luck, the professor asked his four friends to take a rest. "I think you need to know exactly what you are looking for, my little ones," the professor said.

Suddenly, the professor had a thought. Only a few minutes had passed in Bethlehem since their last visit, so his cellphone would still have his fresh scent on it.

The professor then removed the belt from his shepherd costume, and let each of his four friends take a good whiff. "Now that you have my scent my little ones, go find my phone!" the professor commanded.

Within moments, all four of the professor's friends were focused on the same spot in the sand. He knelt down and quickly began digging.

To his pure joy and delight, after only a couple of minutes of digging, he found his phone. "This is a Christmas miracle!" the professor exclaimed to his friends. "I cannot believe that we have found my cellphone!"

"Thank you my Lily, Benji, Karat and Jem! Because of you, we can now return home knowing that the true meaning of Christmas will forever remain a matter of faith. When we get home, I will see to it that my phone is destroyed."

The professor knew that it was time to return home. In a few minutes, his time machine would carry the five of them home. So he gathered his four friends around him, and they waited together on the desert sand. After a few minutes, Professor McDougal's time machine, having worked once again, transported the Christmas time travelers safely home.

The lights of the time machine flashed as the travelers found themselves back in the safety of the professor's home.

The professor slowly opened the heavy metal door of his machine, and they all stepped out into the living room.

The house had grown cold while the five friends were away, so the professor gathered some kindling, placed it in the fireplace along with a few logs and lit it. In a few moments, a roaring fire was warming the house.

Exhausted from their third time journey to Bethlehem, Lily, Benji, Karat and Jem fell fast asleep in front of the fire.

After collapsing on the sofa, the professor suddenly remembered why they had taken another journey to Bethlehem.

He jumped up and quickly began searching for the newspaper and headline that had caused all the commotion. He found it folded over and tucked under the sofa cushion that he was sitting on. With a sense of great urgency, he unfolded the newspaper to reveal the headline.

To his surprise and wonder, the headline of The Coventry Gazette was completely changed.

The same newspaper that only a few hours earlier reported that the remains of a present day cellphone were found in an excavation outside of Bethlehem, now boasted a headline that read the following:

"The spirit of Christmas is alive and well. Coventry, Bethlehem and the world to celebrate."

With that, the professor sat back in his sofa, smiled gently at his four friends cuddled by the fire and let out a huge sigh of relief.

However, before he could completely relax and settle down for a long Christmas Eve sleep, Professor McDougal took the cellphone from his pocket, removed the battery and placed the phone into the fireplace.

After only a few minutes, it melted into a glowing blob of plastic, metal and glass. Any chance of the photos that he had taken surviving, was now gone forever.

As the fire slowly burned itself out, the professor gathered his four friends together and lead them to his bedroom for a long, well deserved sleep.

Christmas morning arrived and brought with it a beautiful sunrise and a fresh blanket of snow covering the ground.

After the professor returned from Christmas Mass, the five friends spent the entire day together.

While resting in his living room on Christmas night, Professor McDougal began thinking about everything that happened the night before. He reminded himself that everything we do should be done for the glory of God, not for our own personal glory or gain. As he had come to realize two years before, PROOF DENIES FAITH. He had succeeded in keeping the birth of Jesus a matter of hope and faith. His amazing time machine had saved the day, along with the helping paws and snouts of his fellow time travelers, Lily, Benji, Karat and Jem.

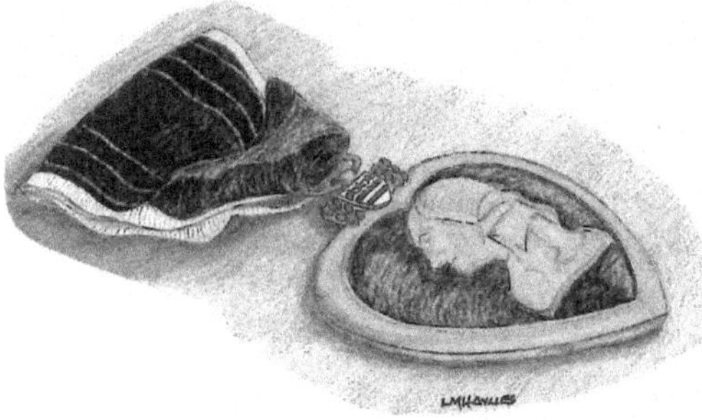

Whatever you do, do all things for the glory of God.

1 Corinthians 10:31 (NIV)

About the Author

Laurence M. Haynes is a licensed land surveyor whose hobbies include music, sports and illustration. His interest in and love of illustration, combined with wanting to influence the lives of young people in a faith-filled, positive way has lead to the creation of this book and eight previously published books titled The Christmas Time Travelers 1, The Littlest Patriots, The Vanishing Doorknob, The Magical Christmas Tree, Legacies, The Christmas Time Travelers 2, The Runaway Clock and The Empty Christmas Stocking. The father of three adult daughters, Catherine, Christina and Bernadette, and grandfather to Ellie and Luca, Larry is an active member of St. Edward the Confessor Parish in Syosset, N.Y., where he and his lovely wife Amy reside.

Visit Larry's web-site@ lmhaynesbooks.com

In loving memory of
Sandra Jaclyn Bruns